ABCDE
FGHIJK
LMNOP
QRSTU
VWXYZ

Michael Hall

Swing

Greenwillow Books

An Imprint of HarperCollins Publishers

The first letter was alone
when a second letter arrived.
"Can I play with you?" the second letter asked.

The second letter was different.

Unlike the first letter, who lived
in the middle of the alphabet,
the second letter lived at the far end.

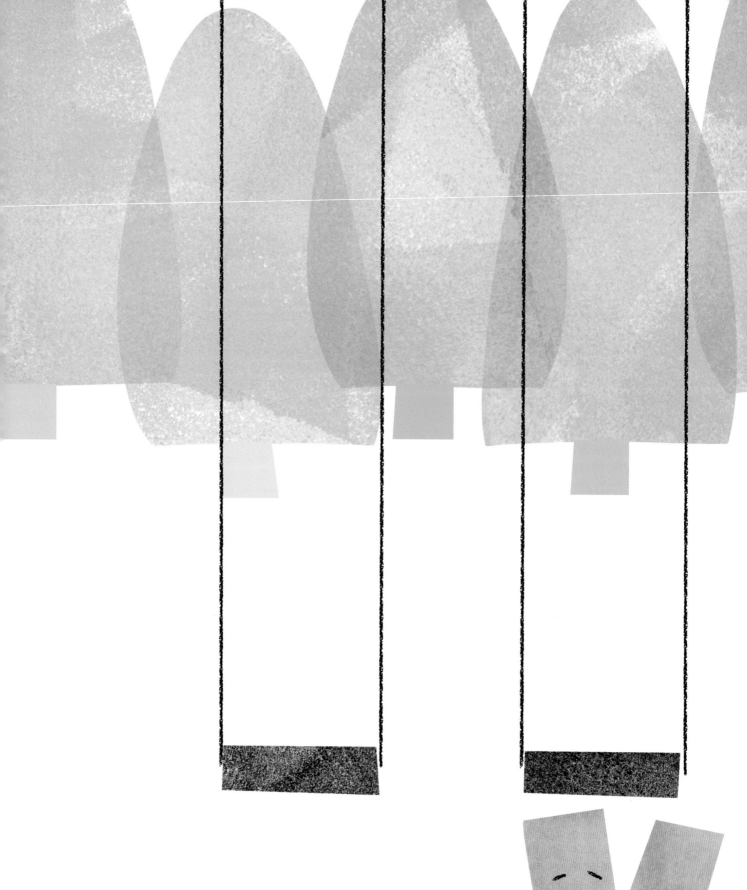

"I'm sorry," said the first letter.
"These swings are saved for
letters from my neighborhood."

Then a third letter came by.
"Can I play with you?"
the third letter asked.

The third letter was different.

Unlike the first two letters,
the third letter was a member
of a small group called vowels.

"I'm sorry," said the second letter.
"Vowels are not allowed
on these swings."

Then a fourth letter appeared.
"Can I play with you?"
the fourth letter asked.

The fourth letter was different.

Unlike the first three letters,
who were made up of straight lines,
the fourth letter was round.

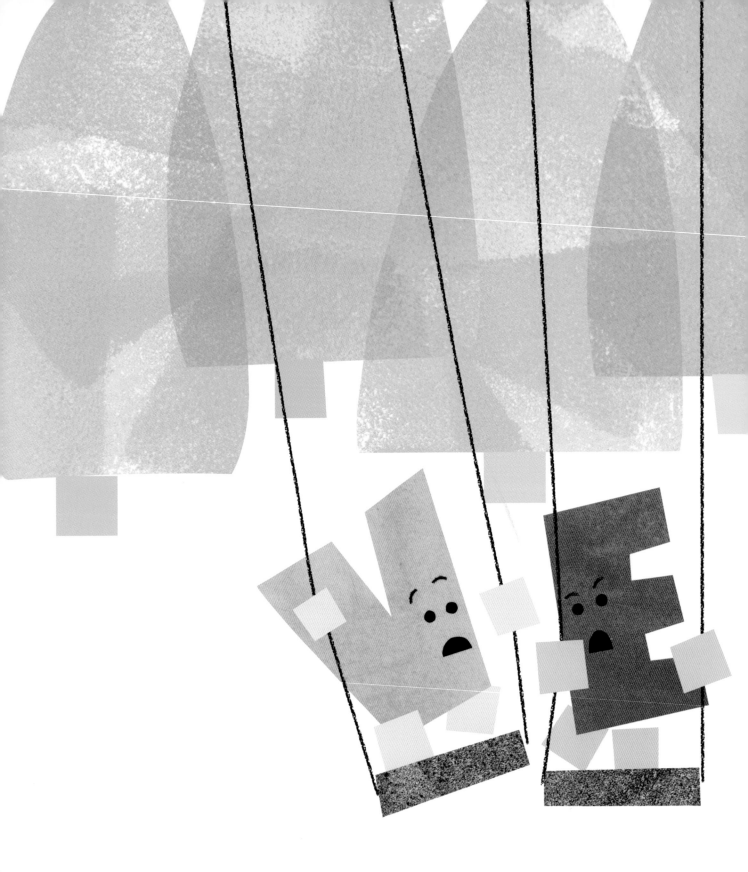

"I'm sorry," said the third letter.

"These swings are saved for–Ouch!

You bumped me!"

"Did not," said the second letter.

"Did too," said the third letter.

"Did too," said the first letter.

While the first three letters tussled,
the fourth letter climbed onto a swing.
"Hey!" said the second letter.

The first three letters
scrambled for
the open swings.

"I wanted that swing!"
said the second letter.
"Too bad," said the third letter.

"Hey, I have an idea," said the fourth letter.

"Let's just swing!"

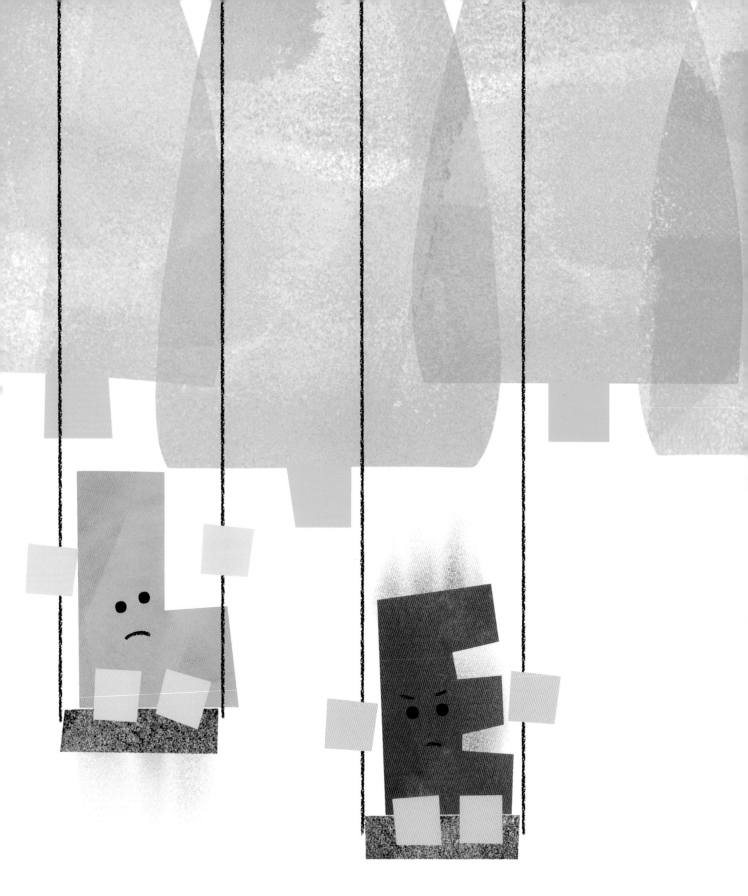

And they did.

Up
and
down.

Back
and
forth.

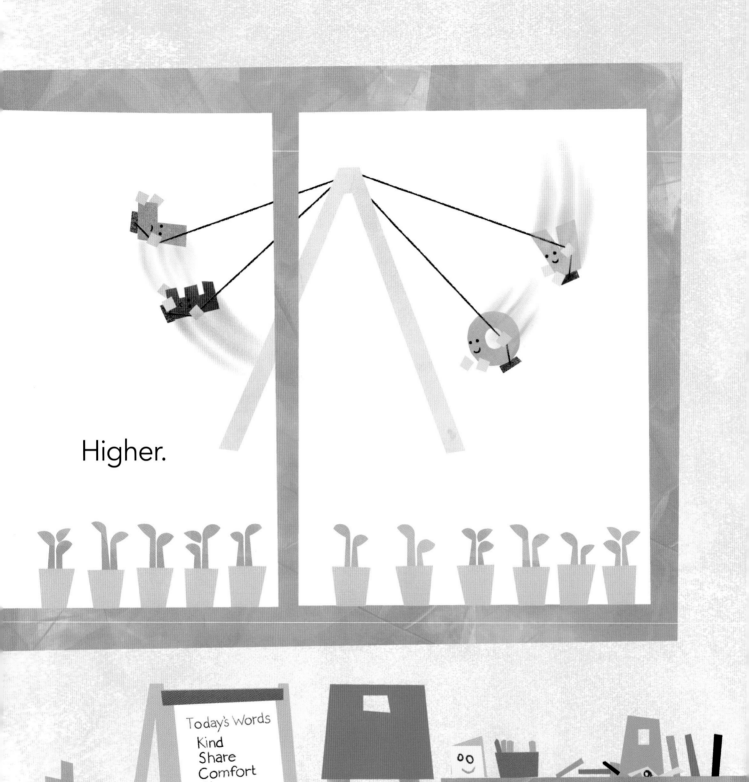

Higher.

Where do you live?

ABCDEFGHI

Alpha Heights

JKLMNOPQR

Middle Town

STUVWXYZ

Far End

Vowels rock!

AEIOU Y

And sometimes

Round or straight lines?

AFHKLNTWX
EIMVYZ

Straight
lines

JPDBG
UPRBQ

Straight and
round lines

CO
S

Round
lines

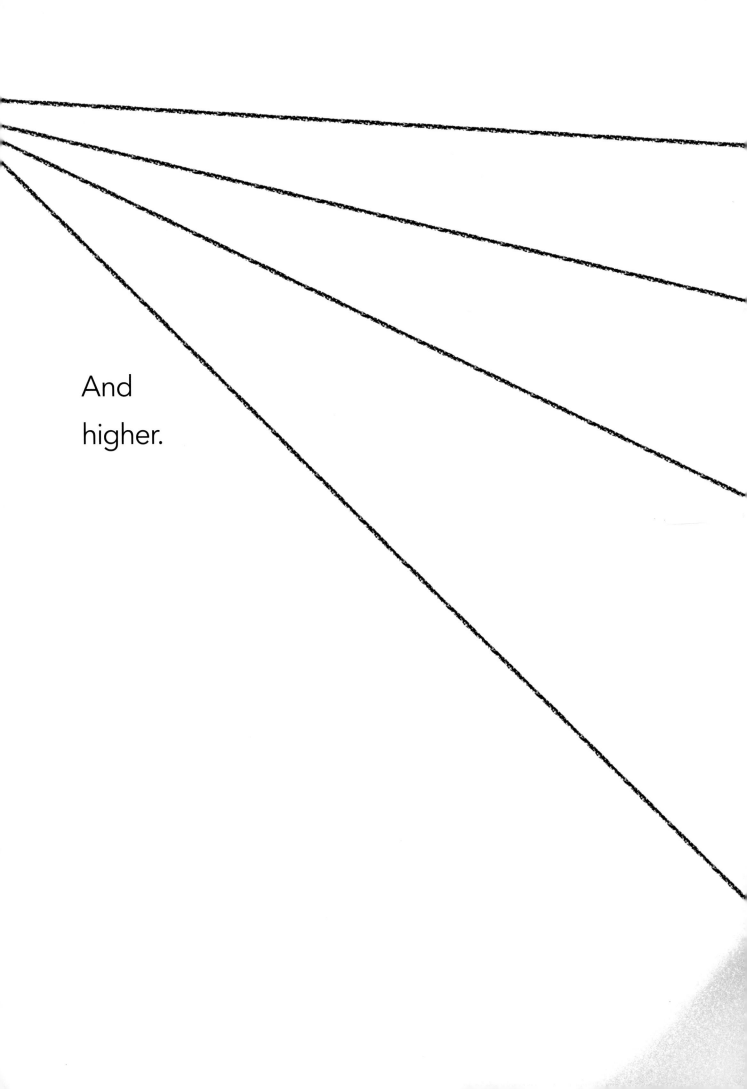

And

higher.

And
higher.

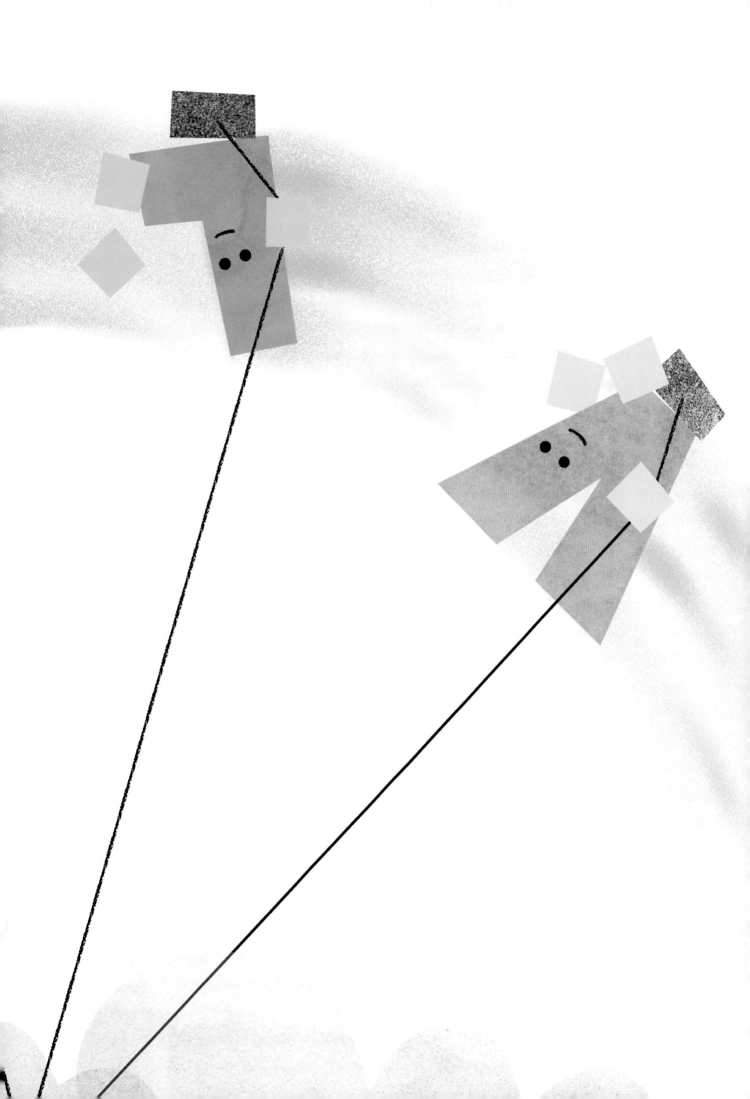

Until their tummies
were laughing,

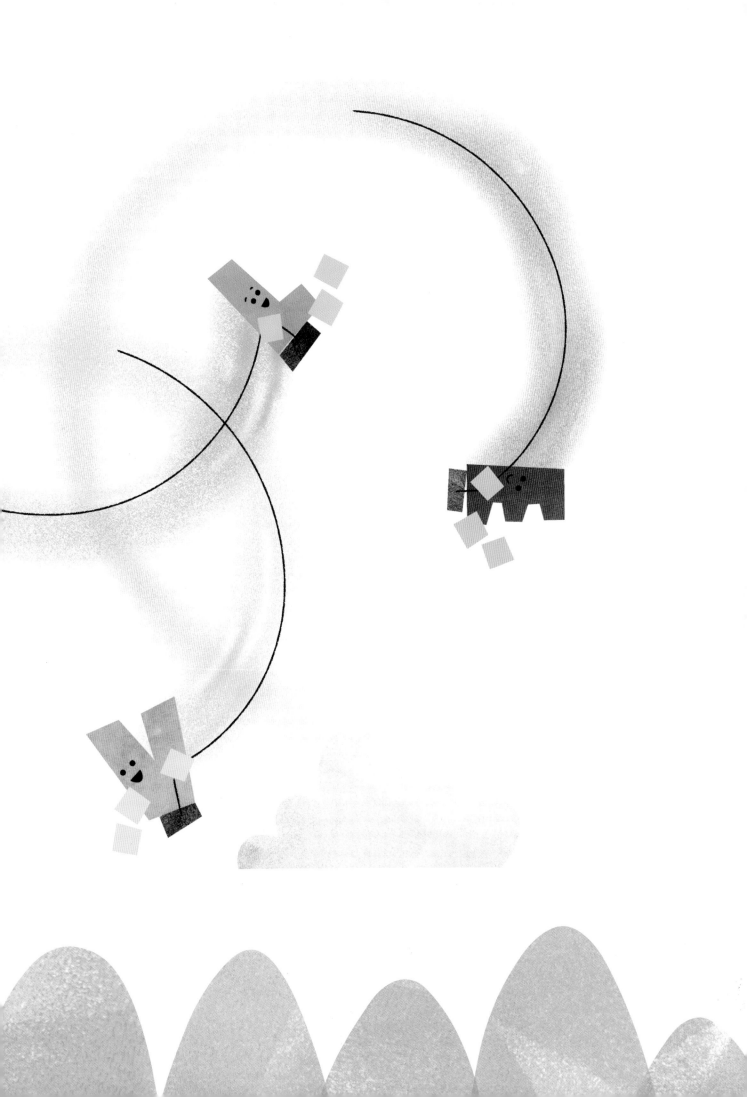

and their hearts

were cheering.

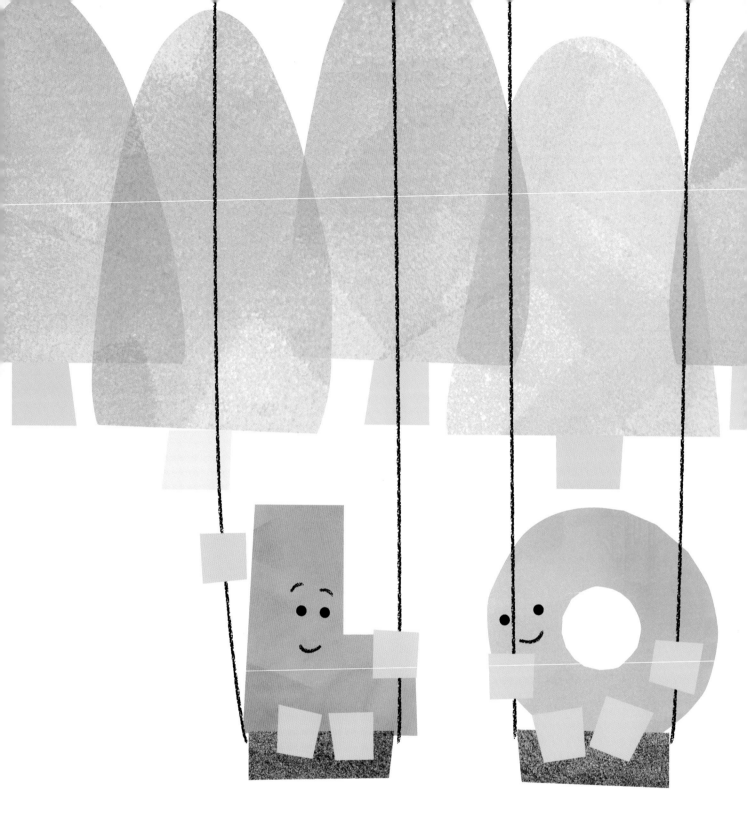

When they landed, they were different.

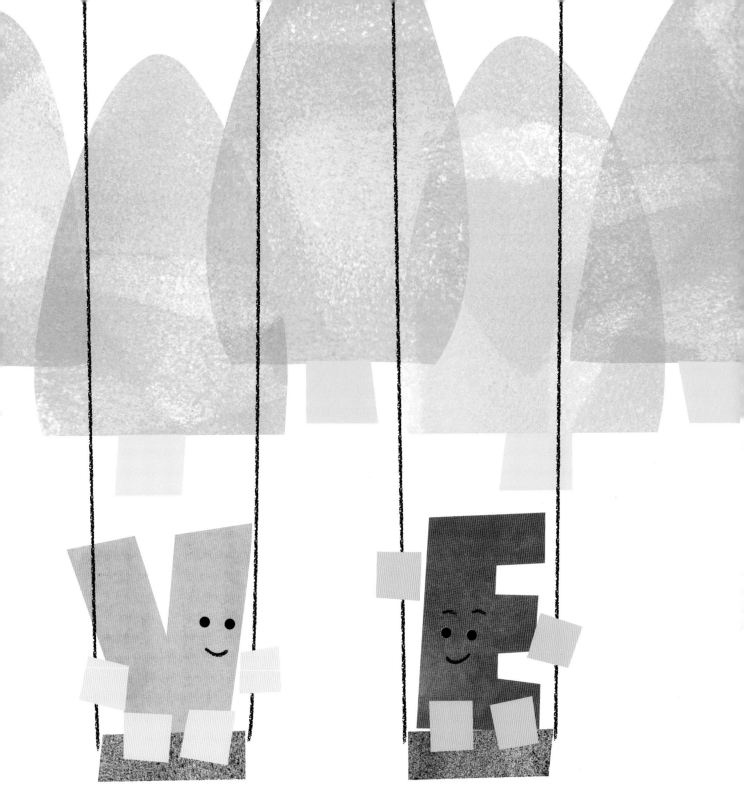

The first letter was on the first swing,
the second letter was on the third swing,
the third letter was on the fourth swing,
and the fourth letter was on the second swing.
And the first letter said . . .

"Let's do it again!"

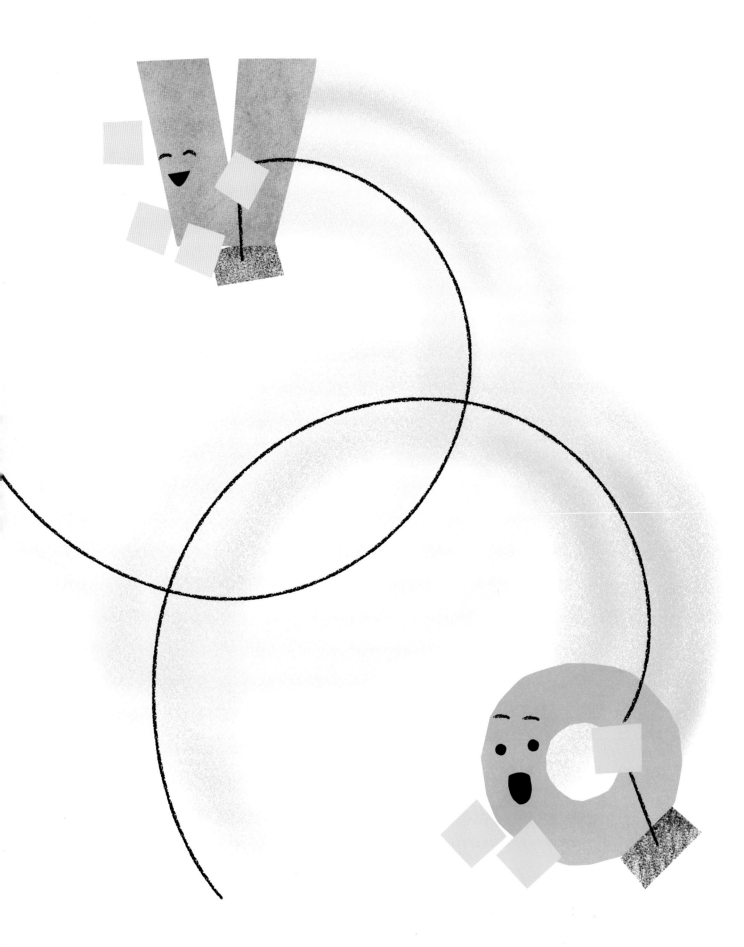

For Bill Guthe

The art is composed of painted paper
and digitally produced line art and shapes.

The text type is 22-point Avenir Next.

Library of Congress Cataloging-in-Publication Data

Names: Hall, Michael, author, illustrator.
Title: Swing / Michael Hall.

Description: First edition. |
New York, NY : Greenwillow Books,
an imprint of HarperCollinsPublishers, [2020] |
Audience: Ages 4-8. | Audience: Grades K-1. |
Summary: As four very different letters arrive at the playground,
each makes the next feel unwelcome,
but once they begin to swing together,
they have a wonderful time.

Identifiers: LCCN 2019041848 | ISBN 9780062866172 (hardcover)

Subjects: CYAC: Social acceptance—Fiction. |
Belonging (Social psychology)—Fiction. |
Playgrounds—Fiction.

Classification: LCC PZ7.H1472 Swi 2020 | DDC [E]—dc23
LC record available at https://lccn.loc.gov/2019041848

20 21 22 23 24 SCP 10 9 8 7 6 5 4 3 2 1

First Edition

Greenwillow Books

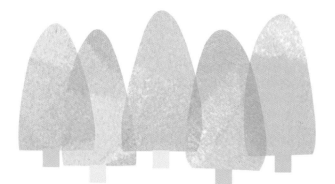